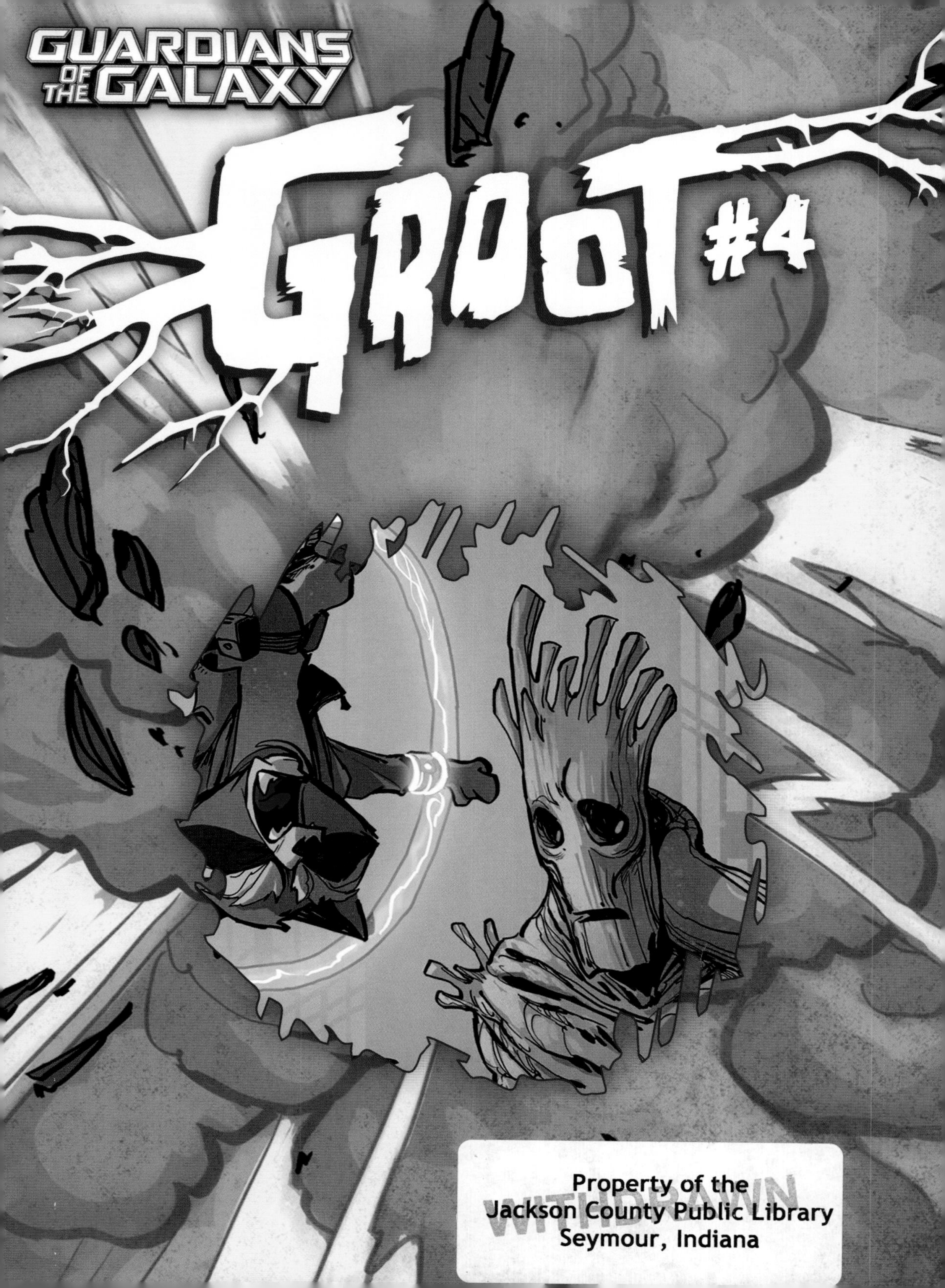
GUARDIANS OF THE GALAXY
GROOT #4

ABDOPUBLISHING.COM

Reinforced library bound edition published in 2018 by Spotlight,
a division of ABDO, PO Box 398166, Minneapolis, Minnesota 55439.
Spotlight produces high-quality reinforced library bound editions for
schools and libraries. Published by agreement with Marvel Characters, Inc.

Printed in the United States of America, North Mankato, Minnesota.
042017
092017

THIS BOOK CONTAINS
RECYCLED MATERIALS

marvelkids.com
© 2017 MARVEL

PUBLISHER'S CATALOGING IN PUBLICATION DATA

Names: Loveness, Jeff, author. | Kesinger, Brian ; Gandini, Vero, illustrators.
Title: Groot / writer: Jeff Loveness ; art: Brian Kesinger ; Vero Gandini.
Description: Reinforced library bound edition. | Minneapolis, Minnesota : Spotlight,
    2018. | Series: Guardians of the galaxy : Groot | Volumes 1, 2, 4, and 6 written
    by Jeff Loveness ; illustrated by Brian Kesinger. | Volumes 3 and 5 written by
    Jeff Loveness ; illustrated by Brian Kesinger & Vero Gandini.
Summary: When Rocket and Groot are on an intergalactic road trip, the two get
    separated and it's up to Groot to help his friend. Whatever comes this famous
    talking-tree-thing's way, one thing's for sure... it's going to be a Groot
    adventure!
Identifiers: LCCN 2017931596 | ISBN 9781532140778 (#1) | ISBN 9781532140785
    (#2) | ISBN 9781532140792 (#3) | ISBN 9781532140808 (#4) | ISBN
    9781532140815 (#5) | ISBN 9781532140822 (#6)
Subjects: LCSH: Superheroes--Juvenile fiction. | Adventure and adventurers--
    Juvenile fiction. | Comic books, strips, etc.--Juvenile fiction. | Graphic novels--
    Juvenile fiction.
Classification: DDC 741.5--dc23
LC record available at https://lccn.loc.gov/2017931596

Spotlight

A Division of ABDO
abdopublishing.com

MARVEL ENTERTAINMENT PROUDLY PRESENTS

GROOT

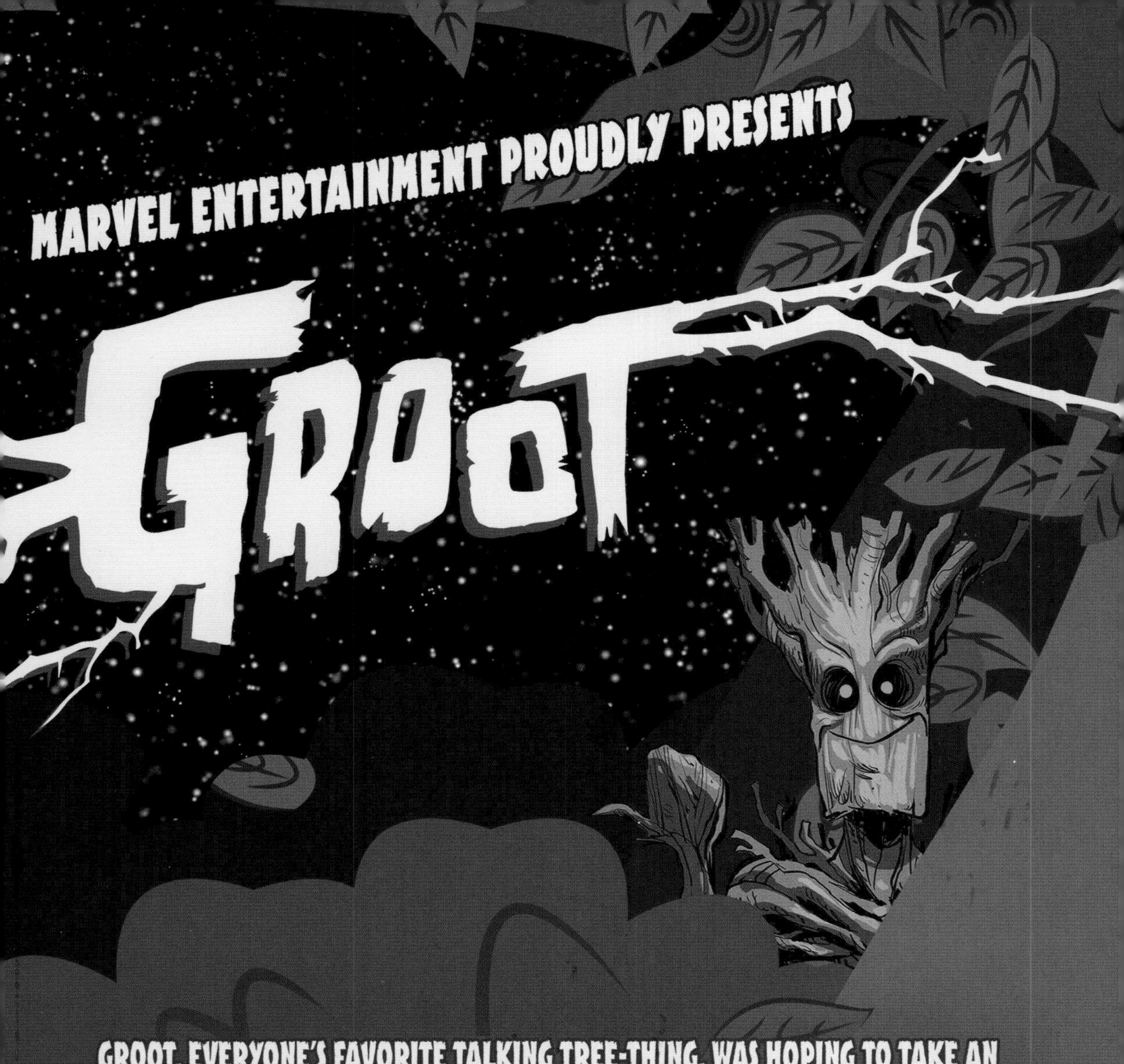

GROOT, EVERYONE'S FAVORITE TALKING TREE-THING, WAS HOPING TO TAKE AN INTERGALACTIC ROADTRIP TO EARTH WITH HIS BEST PAL AND FELLOW GUARDIAN OF THE GALAXY, ROCKET RACCOON.

BUT A DANGEROUS BOUNTY HUNTER NAMED ERIS DERAILED THEIR PLANS, HOPING TO CLAIM A SIZEABLE BOUNTY ON GROOT'S HEAD! SHE HAD TO SETTLE FOR CAPTURING ROCKET, AND IS NOW USING HIM AS BAIT TO LURE GROOT INTO HER CLUTCHES!

JEFF LOVENESS
WRITER

BRIAN KESINGER
ARTIST

JEFF ECKLEBERRY
LETTERER

DECLAN SHALVEY & JORDIE BELLAIRE
COVER ARTISTS

DEVIN LEWIS
EDITOR

SANA AMANAT
SUPERVISING EDITOR

NICK LOWE
SENIOR EDITOR

AXEL ALONSO
EDITOR IN CHIEF

JOE QUESADA
CHIEF CREATIVE OFFICER

DAN BUCKLEY
PUBLISHER

ALAN FINE
EXEC PRODUCER

GROOT CREATED BY STAN LEE, LARRY LIEBER AND JACK KIRBY

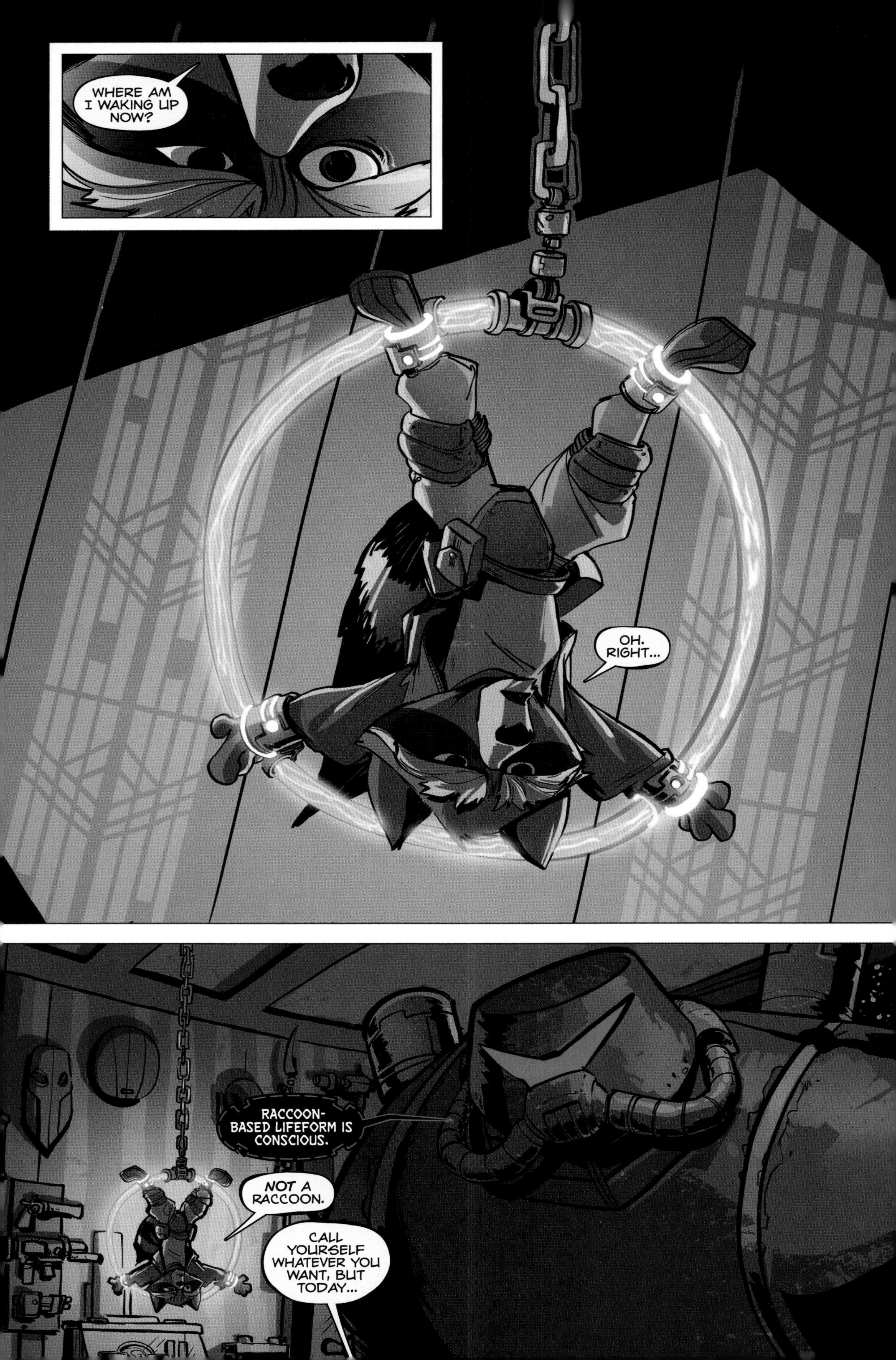
WHERE AM I WAKING UP NOW?
OH. RIGHT...
RACCOON-BASED LIFEFORM IS CONSCIOUS.
NOT A RACCOON.
CALL YOURSELF WHATEVER YOU WANT, BUT TODAY...

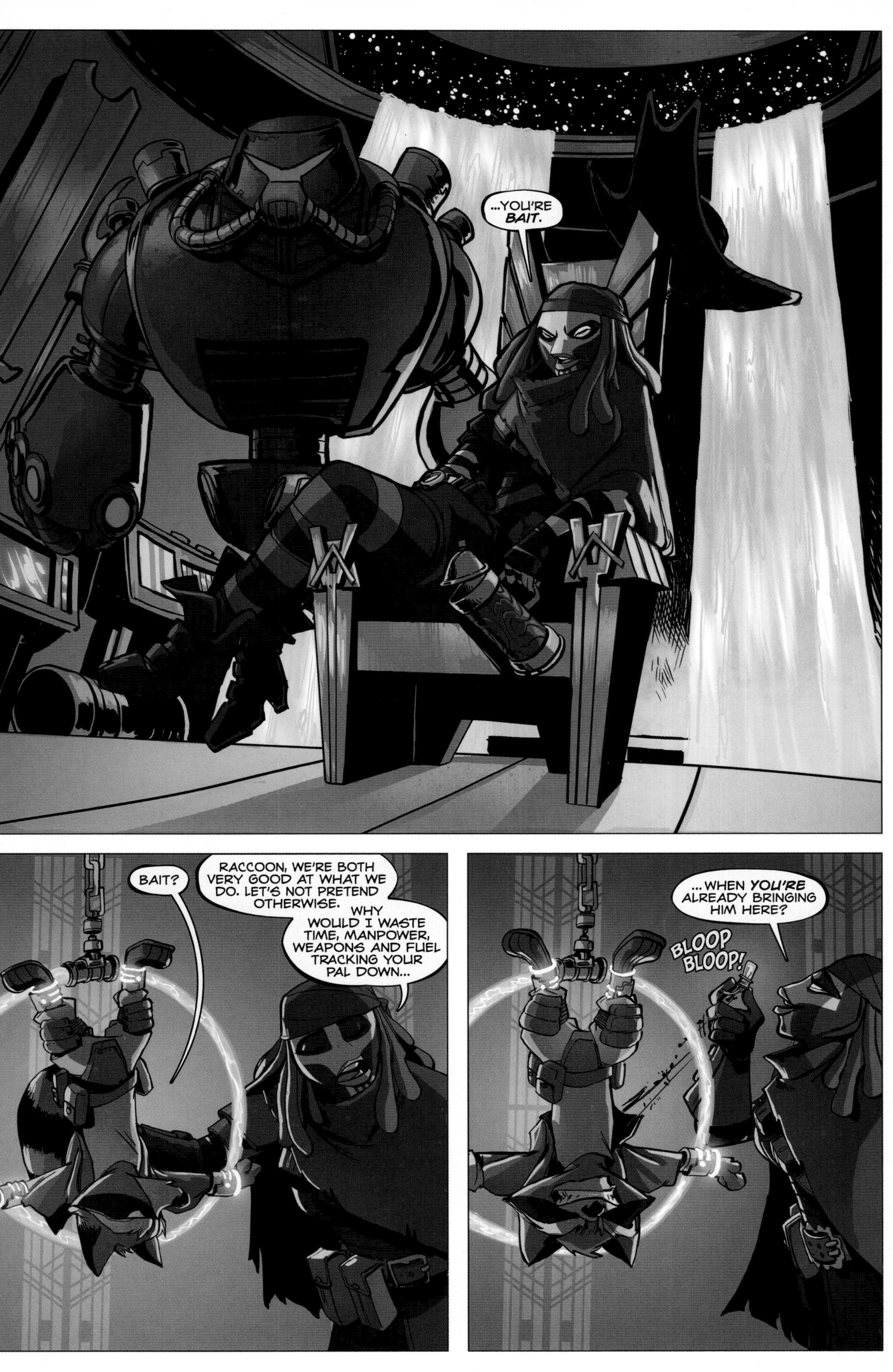
...YOU'RE *BAIT*.
BAIT?
RACCOON, WE'RE BOTH VERY GOOD AT WHAT WE DO. LET'S NOT PRETEND OTHERWISE.
WHY WOULD I WASTE TIME, MANPOWER, WEAPONS AND FUEL TRACKING YOUR PAL DOWN...
...WHEN *YOU'RE* ALREADY BRINGING HIM HERE?
BLOOP BLOOP!

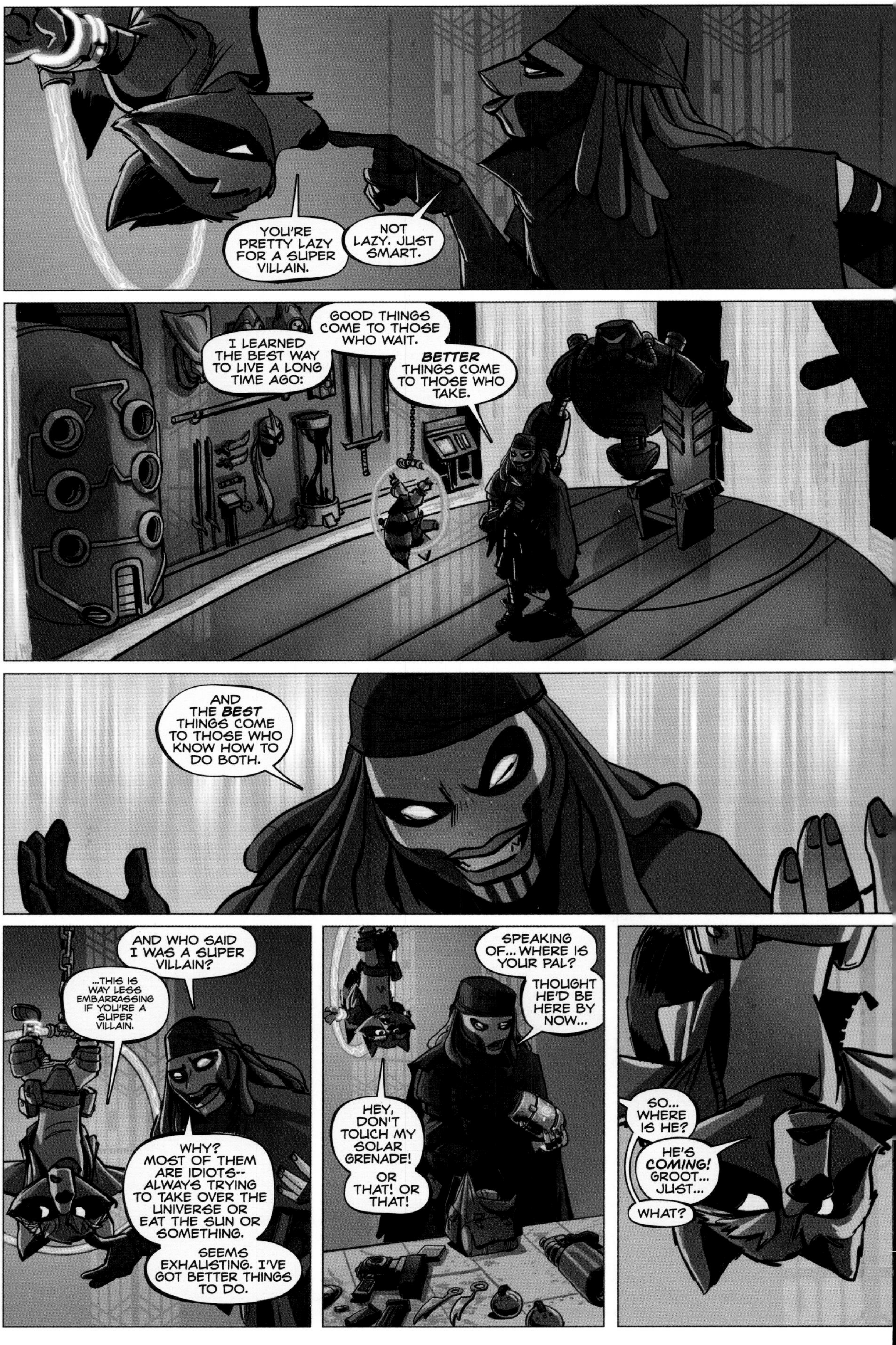

YOU'RE PRETTY LAZY FOR A SUPER VILLAIN.
NOT LAZY. JUST SMART.
I LEARNED THE BEST WAY TO LIVE A LONG TIME AGO:
GOOD THINGS COME TO THOSE WHO WAIT.
BETTER THINGS COME TO THOSE WHO TAKE.
AND THE BEST THINGS COME TO THOSE WHO KNOW HOW TO DO BOTH.
...THIS IS WAY LESS EMBARRASSING IF YOU'RE A SUPER VILLAIN.
AND WHO SAID I WAS A SUPER VILLAIN?
WHY? MOST OF THEM ARE IDIOTS-- ALWAYS TRYING TO TAKE OVER THE UNIVERSE OR EAT THE SUN OR SOMETHING.
SEEMS EXHAUSTING. I'VE GOT BETTER THINGS TO DO.
SPEAKING OF... WHERE IS YOUR PAL?
THOUGHT HE'D BE HERE BY NOW...
HEY, DON'T TOUCH MY SOLAR GRENADE!
OR THAT! OR THAT!
SO... WHERE IS HE?
HE'S COMING! GROOT... JUST...
WHAT?

"GROOT TAKES HIS TIME..."
I AM GROOT.
MAY THE MANTRON PUMP YOUR FUEL?
...IT IS THE MANTRON'S SOLE FUNCTION.
YET...THE MANTRON DREAMS OF GREATER THINGS.
THE MANTRON DREAMS OF SEEING THE STARS.
I AM GROO--
THE MANTRON WAS BUILT TO THE PINNACLE OF EARTHDATE 1996 TECHNOLOGY...
BUT THE MANTRON WAS JETTISONED BY HIS MAKERS.
...TIME HAS FORGOTTEN THE MANTRON.
YET THE MANTRON FEELS HE WAS BUILT FOR SO MUCH MORE.
WE WERE BUILT FOR ONLY ONE THING...

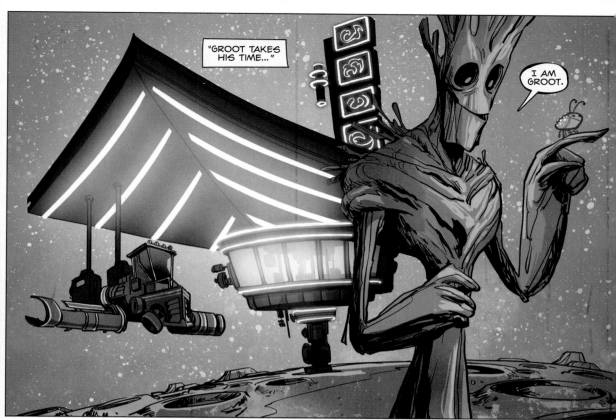

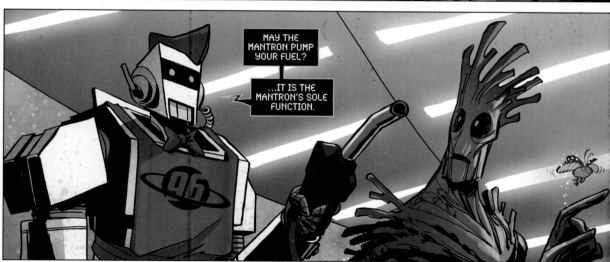

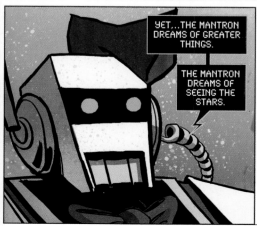

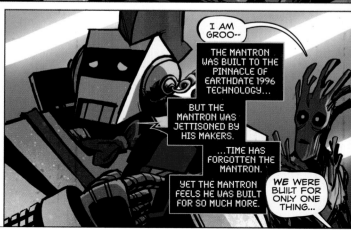

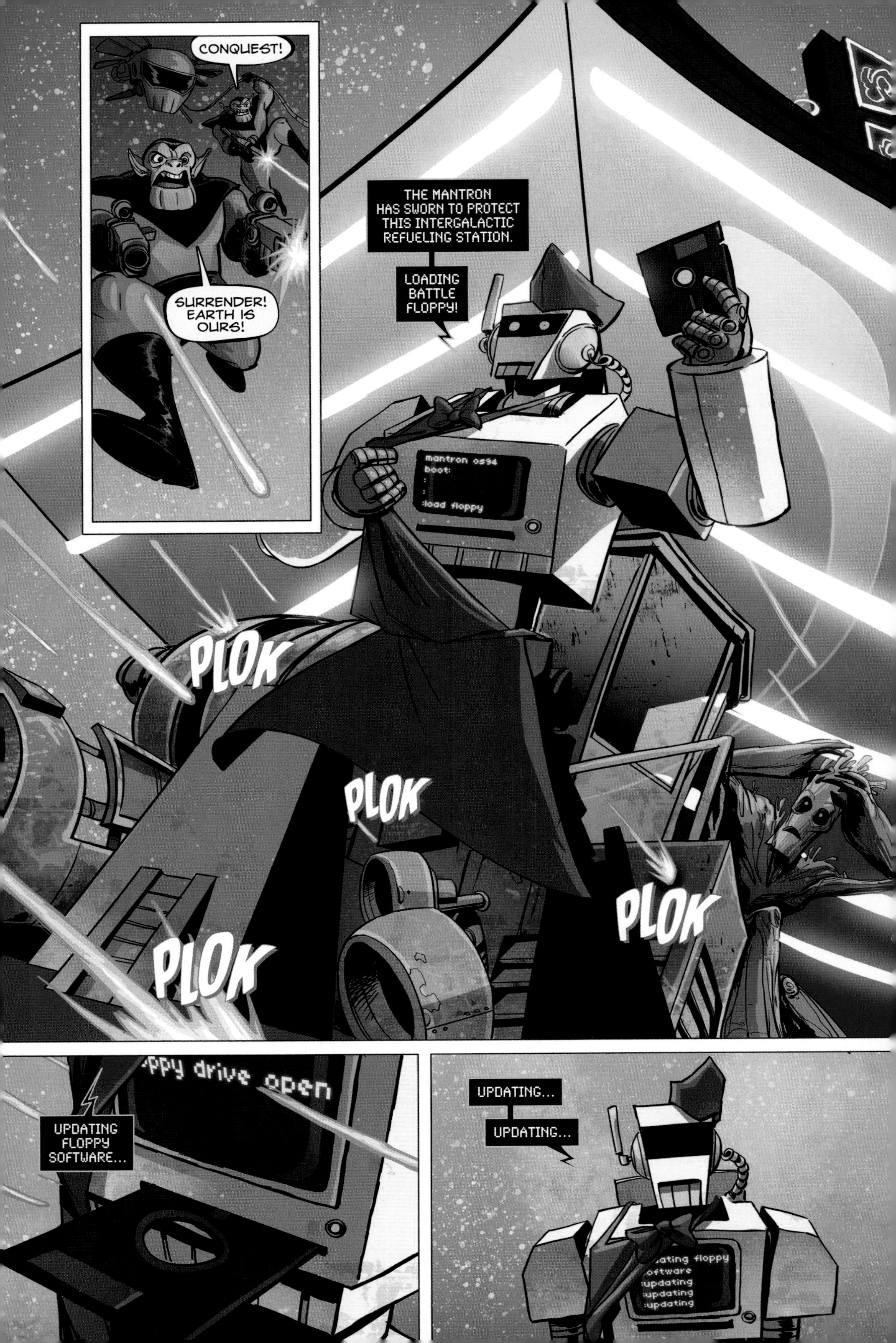
CONQUEST!
SURRENDER! EARTH IS OURS!
THE MANTRON HAS SWORN TO PROTECT THIS INTERGALACTIC REFUELING STATION.
LOADING BATTLE FLOPPY!
mantron os94
boot:
:
:
:load floppy
PLOK
PLOK
PLOK
PLOK
ppy drive open
UPDATING FLOPPY SOFTWARE...
UPDATING...
UPDATING...
dating floppy
oftware
:updating
:updating
:updating

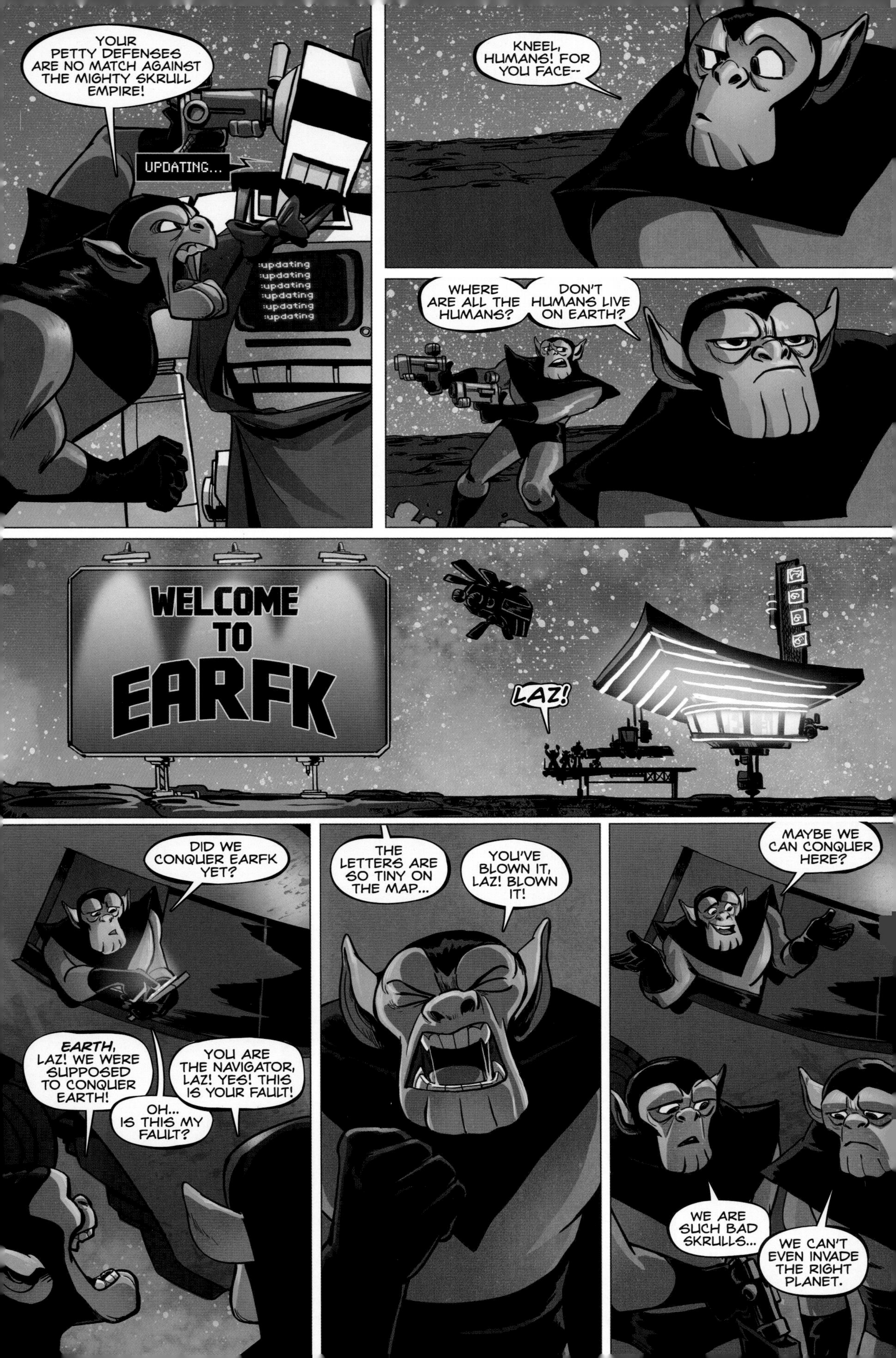
YOUR PETTY DEFENSES ARE NO MATCH AGAINST THE MIGHTY SKRULL EMPIRE!
UPDATING...
:updating
:updating
:updating
:updating
:updating
:updating
KNEEL, HUMANS! FOR YOU FACE--
WHERE ARE ALL THE HUMANS?
DON'T HUMANS LIVE ON EARTH?
WELCOME TO EARFK
LAZ!
DID WE CONQUER EARFK YET?
EARTH, LAZ! WE WERE SUPPOSED TO CONQUER EARTH!
OH... IS THIS MY FAULT?
YOU ARE THE NAVIGATOR, LAZ! YES! THIS IS YOUR FAULT!
THE LETTERS ARE SO TINY ON THE MAP...
YOU'VE BLOWN IT, LAZ! BLOWN IT!
MAYBE WE CAN CONQUER HERE?
WE ARE SUCH BAD SKRULLS...
WE CAN'T EVEN INVADE THE RIGHT PLANET.

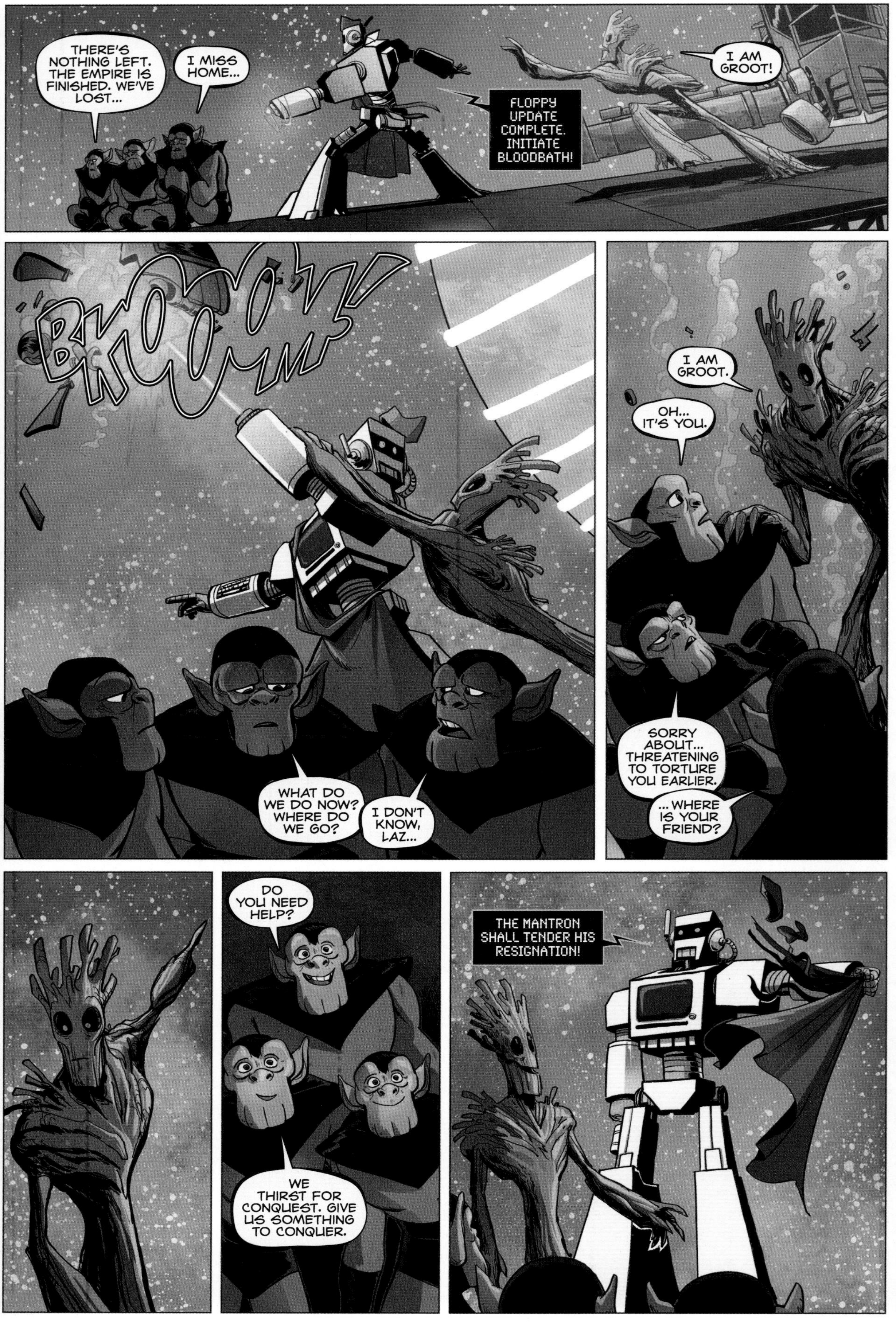
THERE'S NOTHING LEFT. THE EMPIRE IS FINISHED. WE'VE LOST...
I MISS HOME...
FLOPPY UPDATE COMPLETE. INITIATE BLOODBATH!
I AM GROOT!
BKOOOM
WHAT DO WE DO NOW? WHERE DO WE GO?
I DON'T KNOW, LAZ...
I AM GROOT.
OH... IT'S YOU.
SORRY ABOUT... THREATENING TO TORTURE YOU EARLIER.
...WHERE IS YOUR FRIEND?
DO YOU NEED HELP?
WE THIRST FOR CONQUEST. GIVE US SOMETHING TO CONQUER.
THE MANTRON SHALL TENDER HIS RESIGNATION!

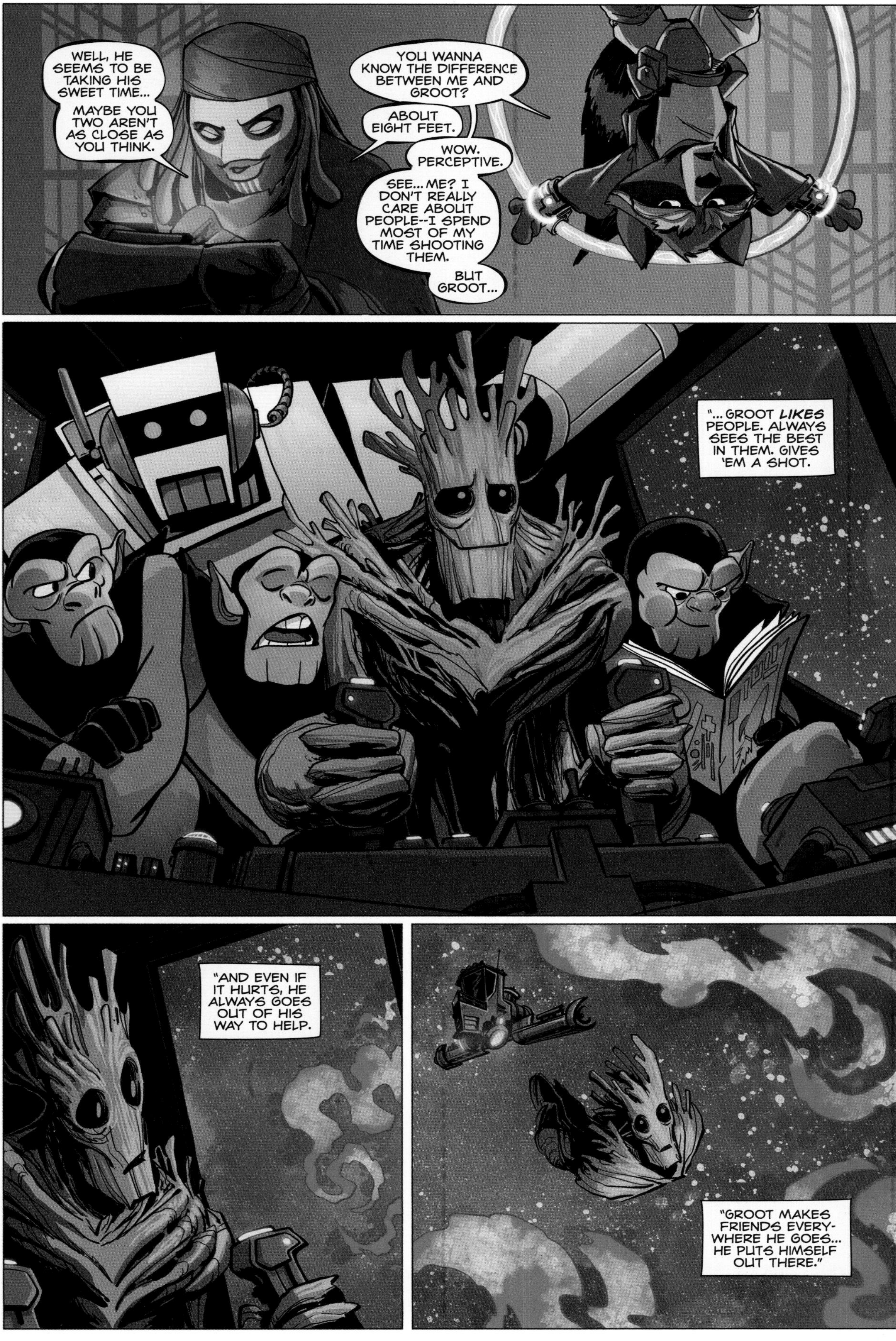
WELL, HE SEEMS TO BE TAKING HIS SWEET TIME...
MAYBE YOU TWO AREN'T AS CLOSE AS YOU THINK.
YOU WANNA KNOW THE DIFFERENCE BETWEEN ME AND GROOT?
ABOUT EIGHT FEET.
WOW. PERCEPTIVE.
SEE... ME? I DON'T REALLY CARE ABOUT PEOPLE--I SPEND MOST OF MY TIME SHOOTING THEM.
BUT GROOT...
"...GROOT LIKES PEOPLE. ALWAYS SEES THE BEST IN THEM. GIVES 'EM A SHOT.
"AND EVEN IF IT HURTS, HE ALWAYS GOES OUT OF HIS WAY TO HELP.
"GROOT MAKES FRIENDS EVERY-WHERE HE GOES... HE PUTS HIMSELF OUT THERE."

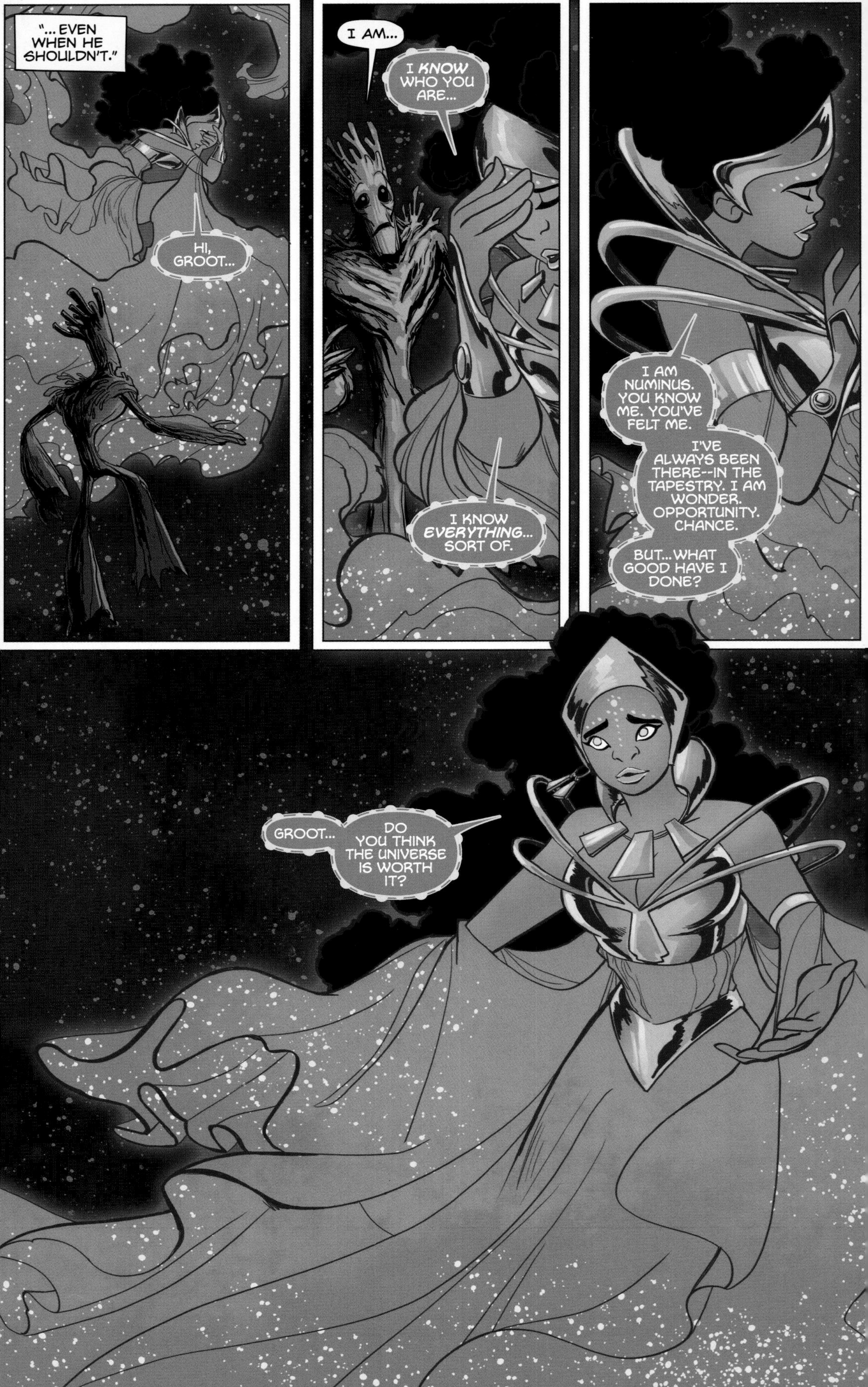
"...EVEN WHEN HE SHOULDN'T."
HI, GROOT...
I AM...
I KNOW WHO YOU ARE...
I KNOW EVERYTHING... SORT OF.
I AM NUMINUS. YOU KNOW ME. YOU'VE FELT ME.
I'VE ALWAYS BEEN THERE--IN THE TAPESTRY. I AM WONDER. OPPORTUNITY. CHANCE.
BUT...WHAT GOOD HAVE I DONE?
GROOT...
DO YOU THINK THE UNIVERSE IS WORTH IT?

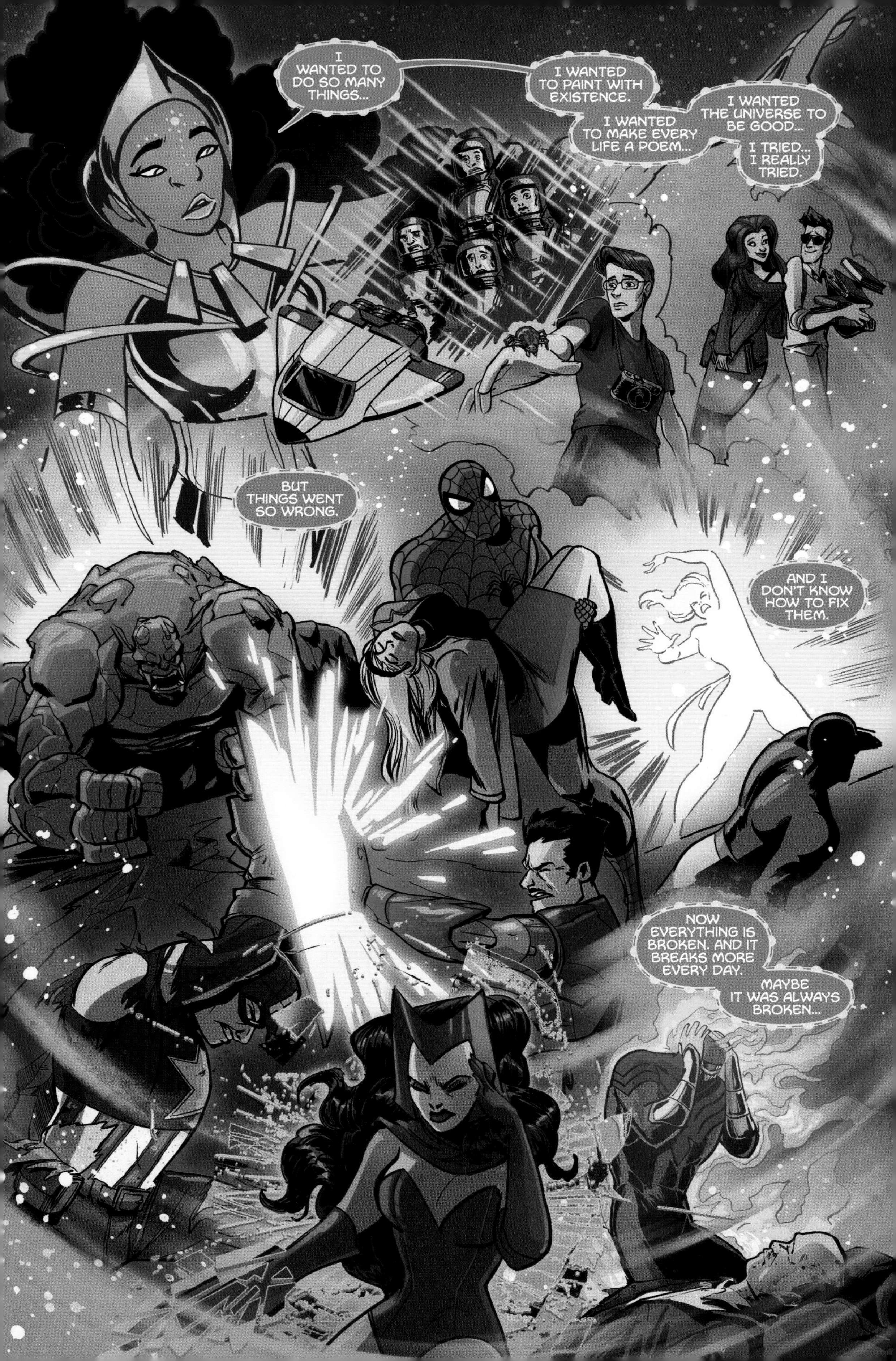

I WANTED TO DO SO MANY THINGS...
I WANTED TO PAINT WITH EXISTENCE.
I WANTED TO MAKE EVERY LIFE A POEM...
I WANTED THE UNIVERSE TO BE GOOD...
I TRIED... I REALLY TRIED.
BUT THINGS WENT SO WRONG.
AND I DON'T KNOW HOW TO FIX THEM.
NOW EVERYTHING IS BROKEN. AND IT BREAKS MORE EVERY DAY.
MAYBE IT WAS ALWAYS BROKEN...

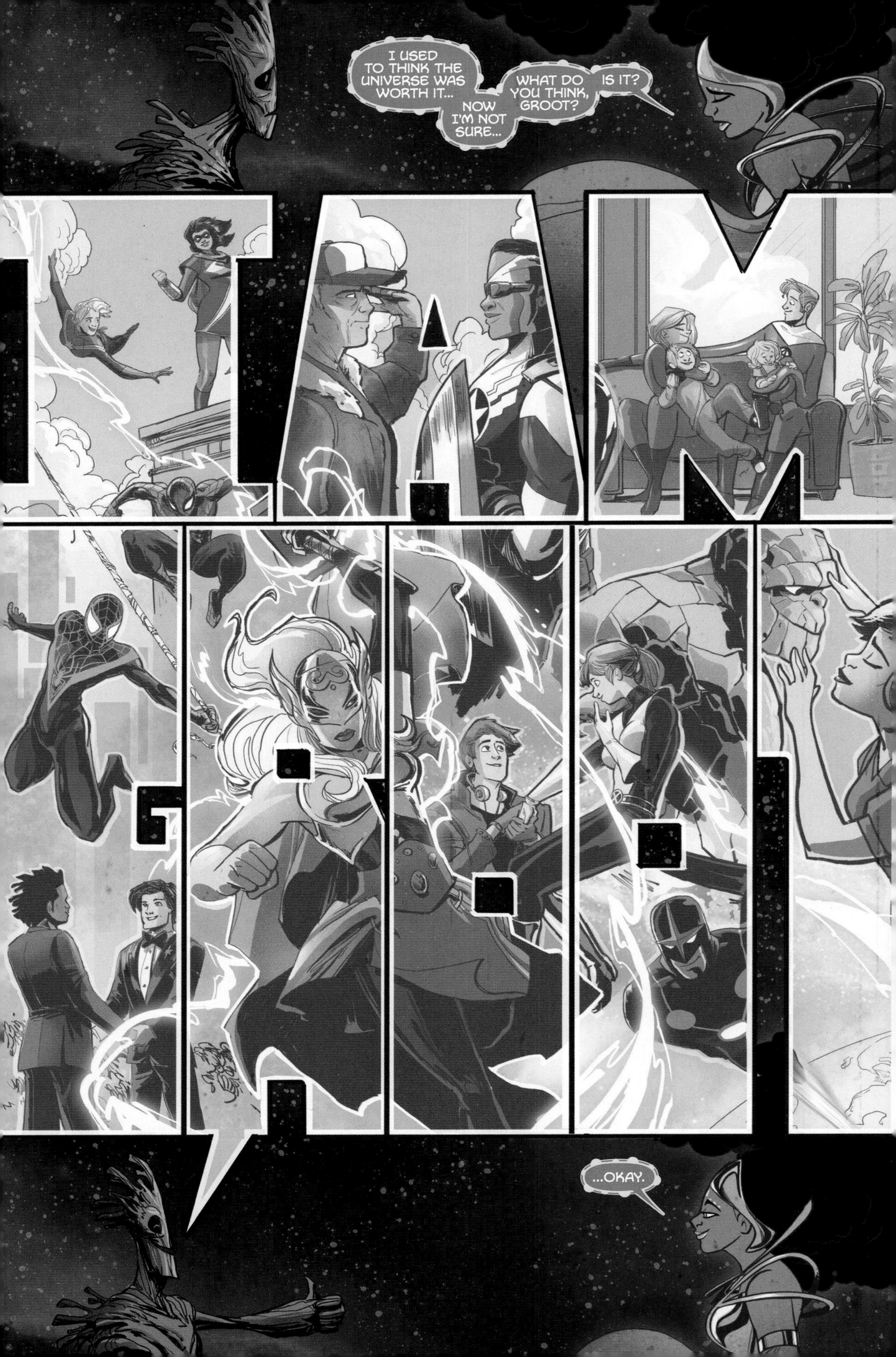
I USED TO THINK THE UNIVERSE WAS WORTH IT...
NOW I'M NOT SURE...
WHAT DO YOU THINK, GROOT?
IS IT?
I AM GROOT
...OKAY.

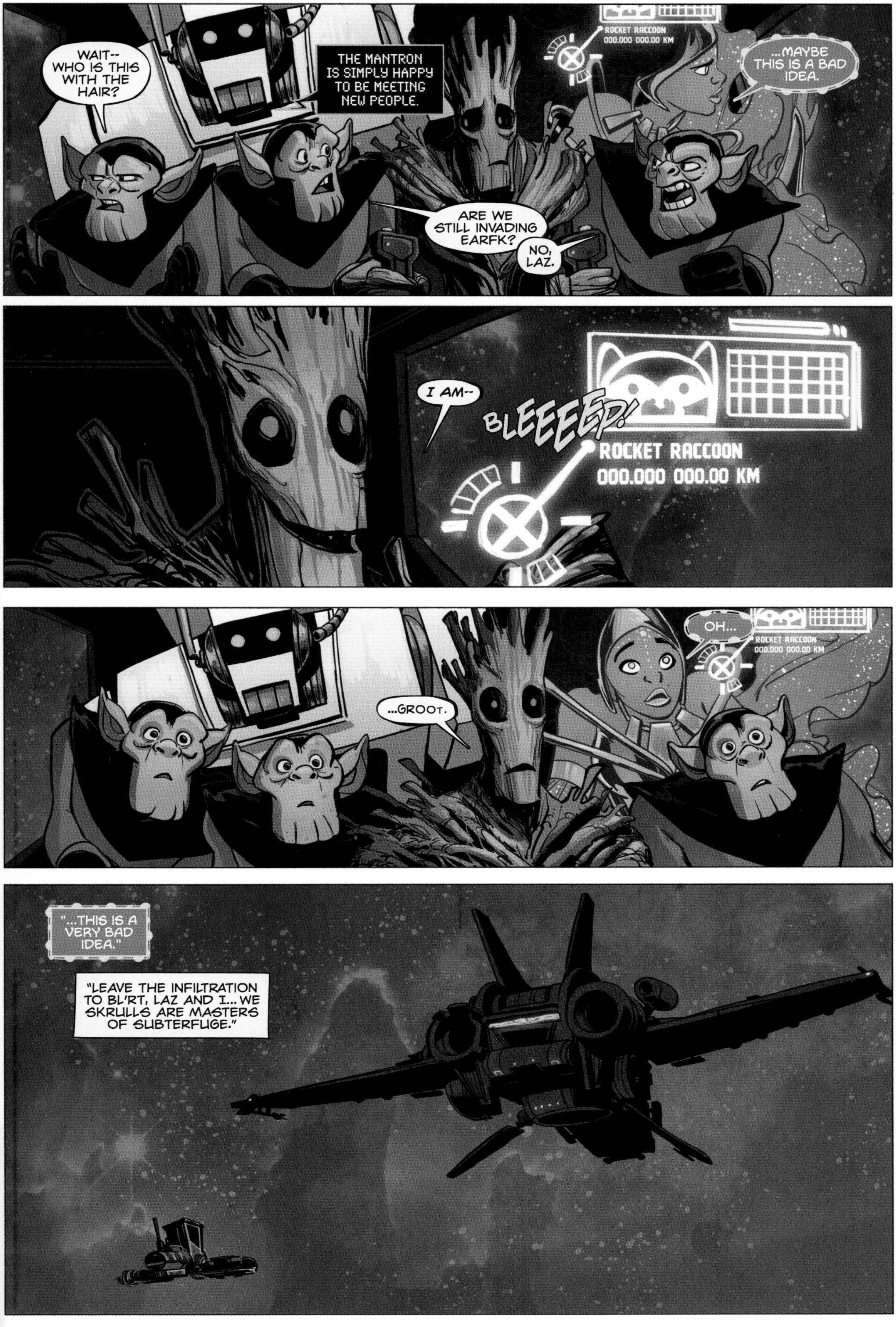
WAIT-- WHO IS THIS WITH THE HAIR?
THE MANTRON IS SIMPLY HAPPY TO BE MEETING NEW PEOPLE.
ROCKET RACCOON 000.000 000.00 KM
...MAYBE THIS IS A BAD IDEA.
ARE WE STILL INVADING EARFK?
NO, LAZ.
I AM--
BLEEEEP!
ROCKET RACCOON 000.000 000.00 KM
OH...
ROCKET RACCOON 000.000 000.00 KM
...GROOT.
"...THIS IS A VERY BAD IDEA."
"LEAVE THE INFILTRATION TO BL'RT, LAZ AND I... WE SKRULLS ARE MASTERS OF SUBTERFUGE."

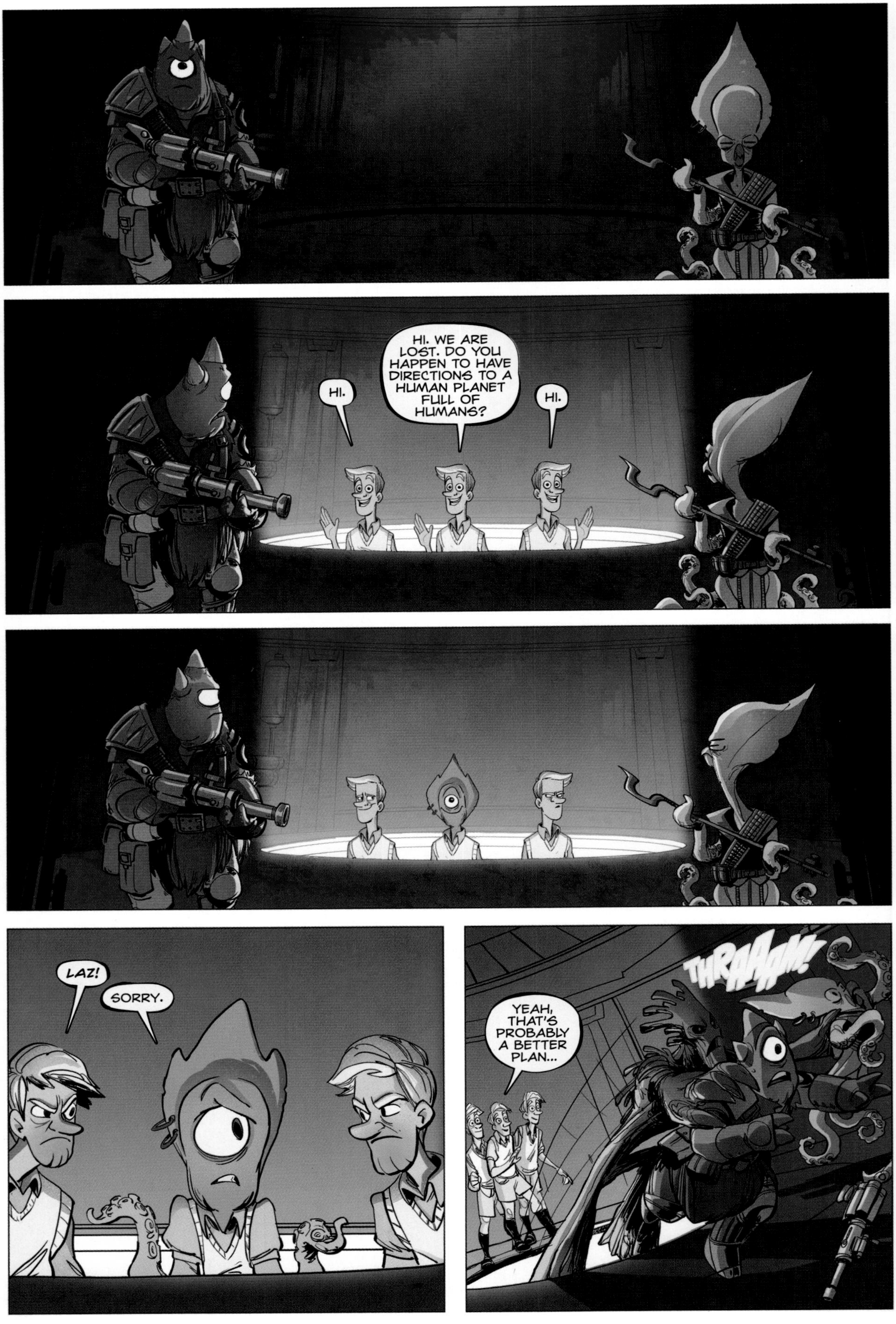
HI.
HI. WE ARE LOST. DO YOU HAPPEN TO HAVE DIRECTIONS TO A HUMAN PLANET FULL OF HUMANS?
HI.
LAZ!
SORRY.
THRAAAM!
YEAH, THAT'S PROBABLY A BETTER PLAN...

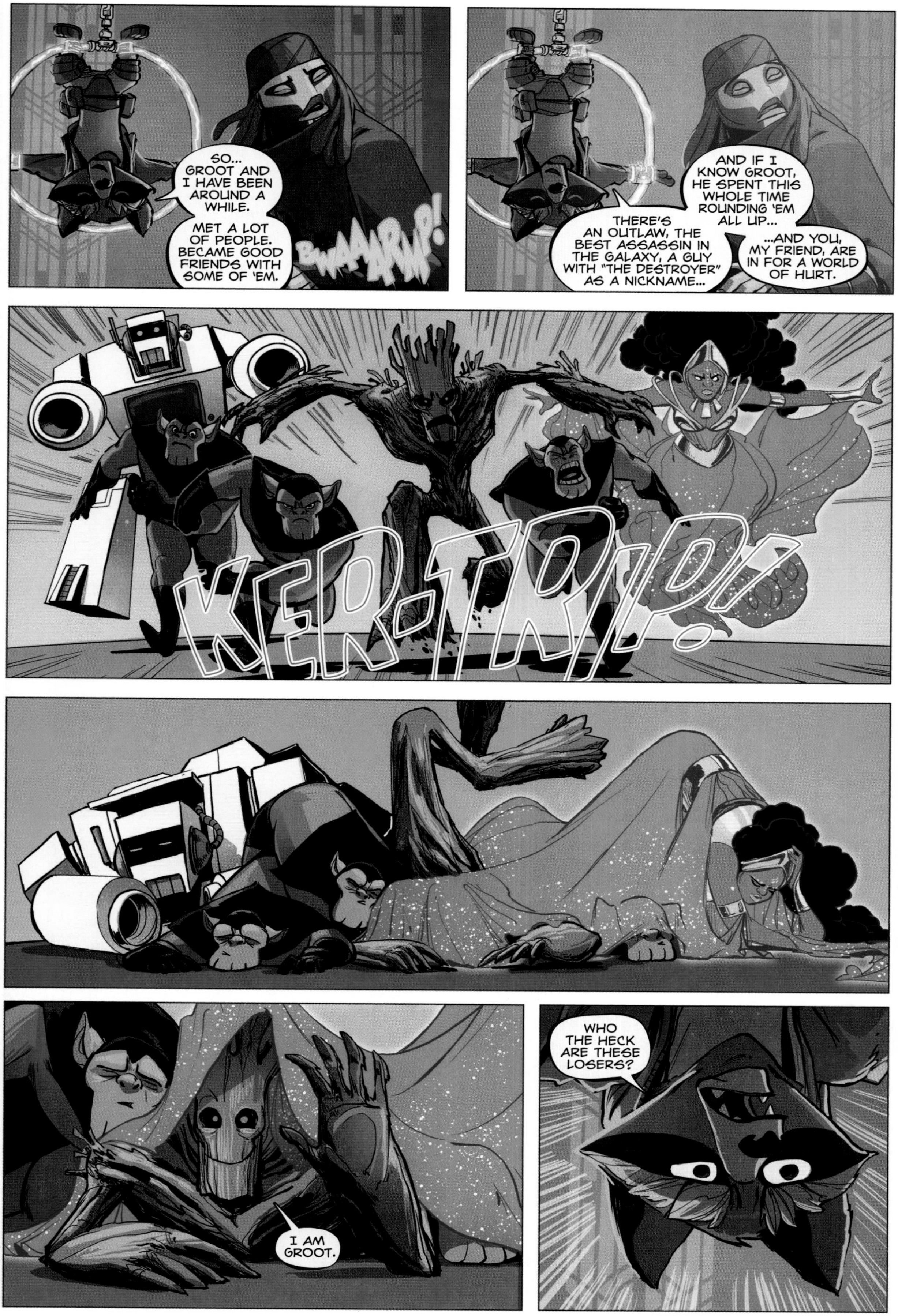
SO... GROOT AND I HAVE BEEN AROUND A WHILE.
MET A LOT OF PEOPLE. BECAME GOOD FRIENDS WITH SOME OF 'EM.
BWAAARMP!
THERE'S AN OUTLAW, THE BEST ASSASSIN IN THE GALAXY, A GUY WITH "THE DESTROYER" AS A NICKNAME...
AND IF I KNOW GROOT, HE SPENT THIS WHOLE TIME ROUNDING 'EM ALL UP...
...AND YOU, MY FRIEND, ARE IN FOR A WORLD OF HURT.
KER-TRIP!
I AM GROOT.
WHO THE HECK ARE THESE LOSERS?

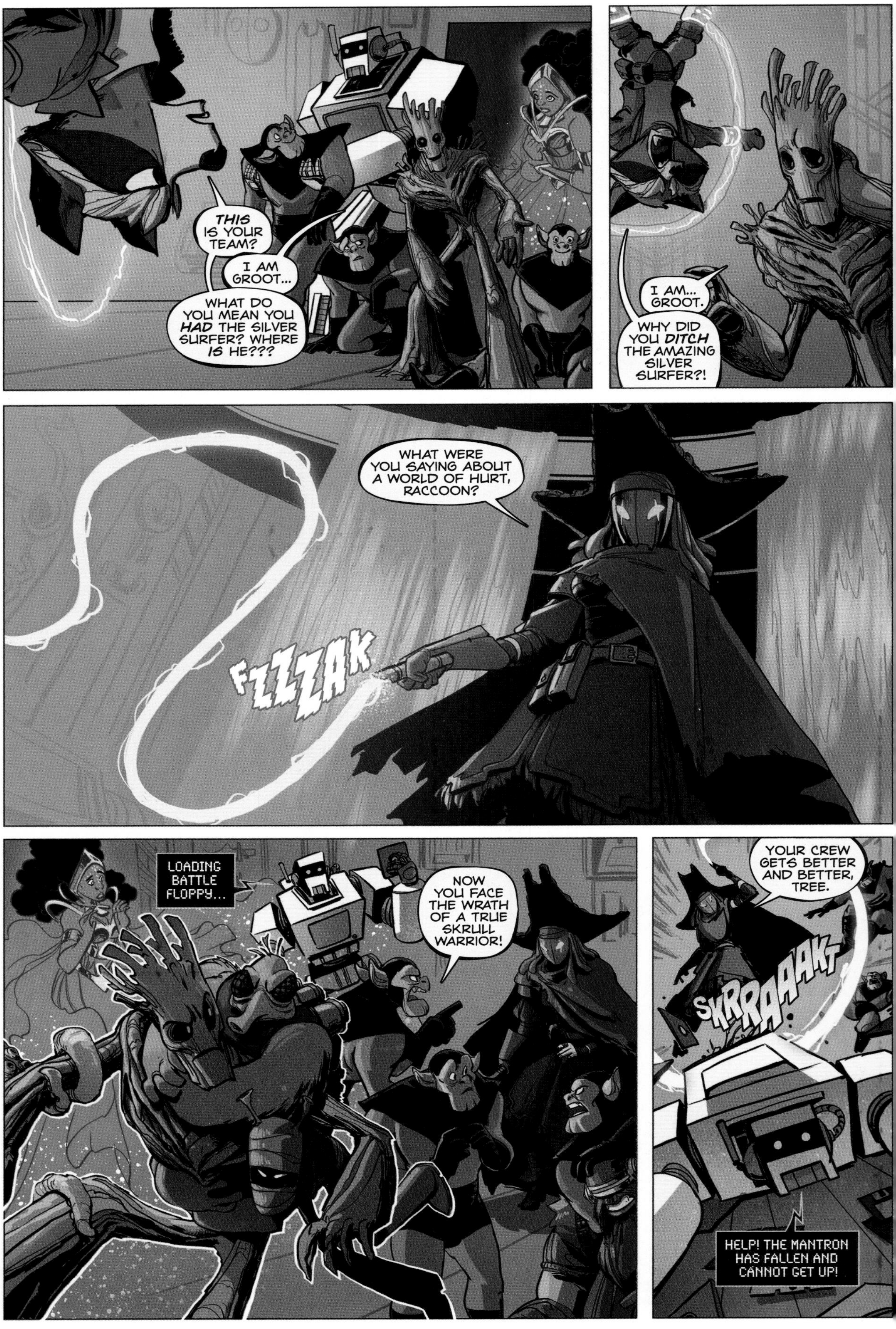
THIS IS YOUR TEAM?
I AM GROOT...
WHAT DO YOU MEAN YOU HAD THE SILVER SURFER? WHERE IS HE???
I AM... GROOT.
WHY DID YOU DITCH THE AMAZING SILVER SURFER?!
WHAT WERE YOU SAYING ABOUT A WORLD OF HURT, RACCOON?
FZZZAK
LOADING BATTLE FLOPPY...
NOW YOU FACE THE WRATH OF A TRUE SKRULL WARRIOR!
YOUR CREW GETS BETTER AND BETTER, TREE.
SKRRAAAKT
HELP! THE MANTRON HAS FALLEN AND CANNOT GET UP!

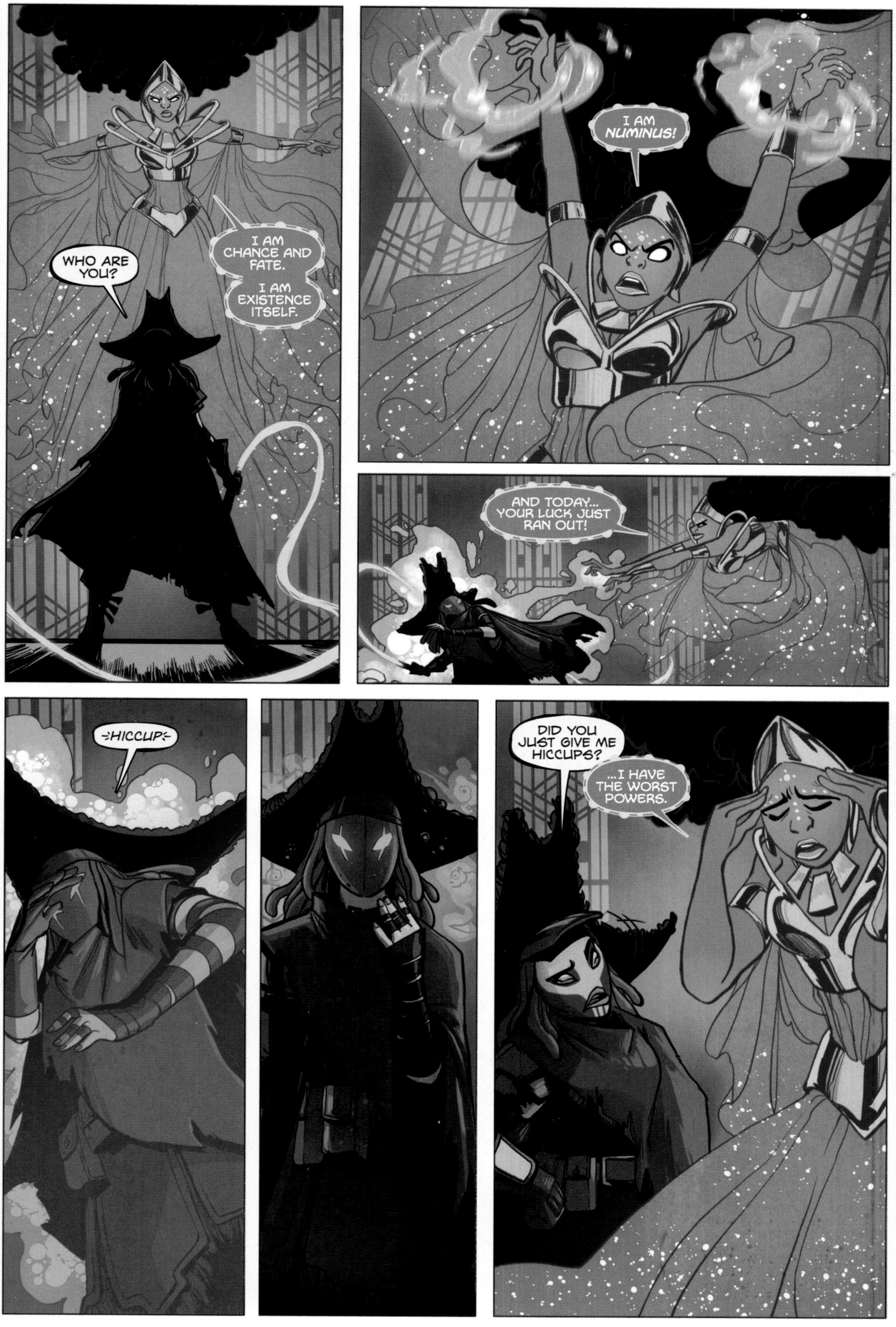

WHO ARE YOU?
I AM CHANCE AND FATE.
I AM EXISTENCE ITSELF.
I AM NUMINUS!
AND TODAY... YOUR LUCK JUST RAN OUT!
HICCUP
DID YOU JUST GIVE ME HICCUPS?
...I HAVE THE WORST POWERS.

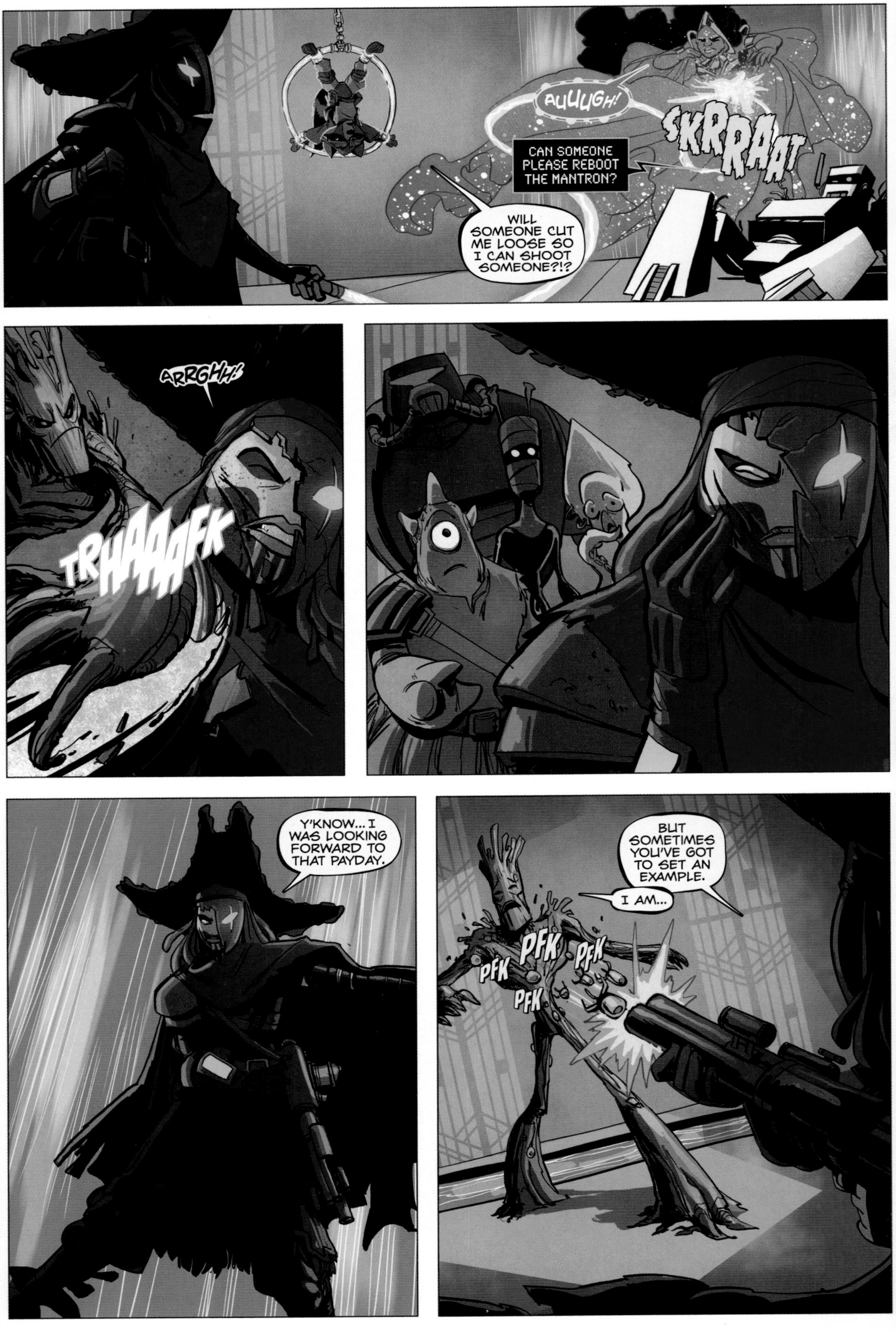
AUUUGH!
SKRRAAT
CAN SOMEONE PLEASE REBOOT THE MANTRON?
WILL SOMEONE CUT ME LOOSE SO I CAN SHOOT SOMEONE?!?
ARRGHH!
TRHAAAAFK
Y'KNOW... I WAS LOOKING FORWARD TO THAT PAYDAY.
BUT SOMETIMES YOU'VE GOT TO SET AN EXAMPLE.
I AM...
PFK
PFK
PFK
PFK

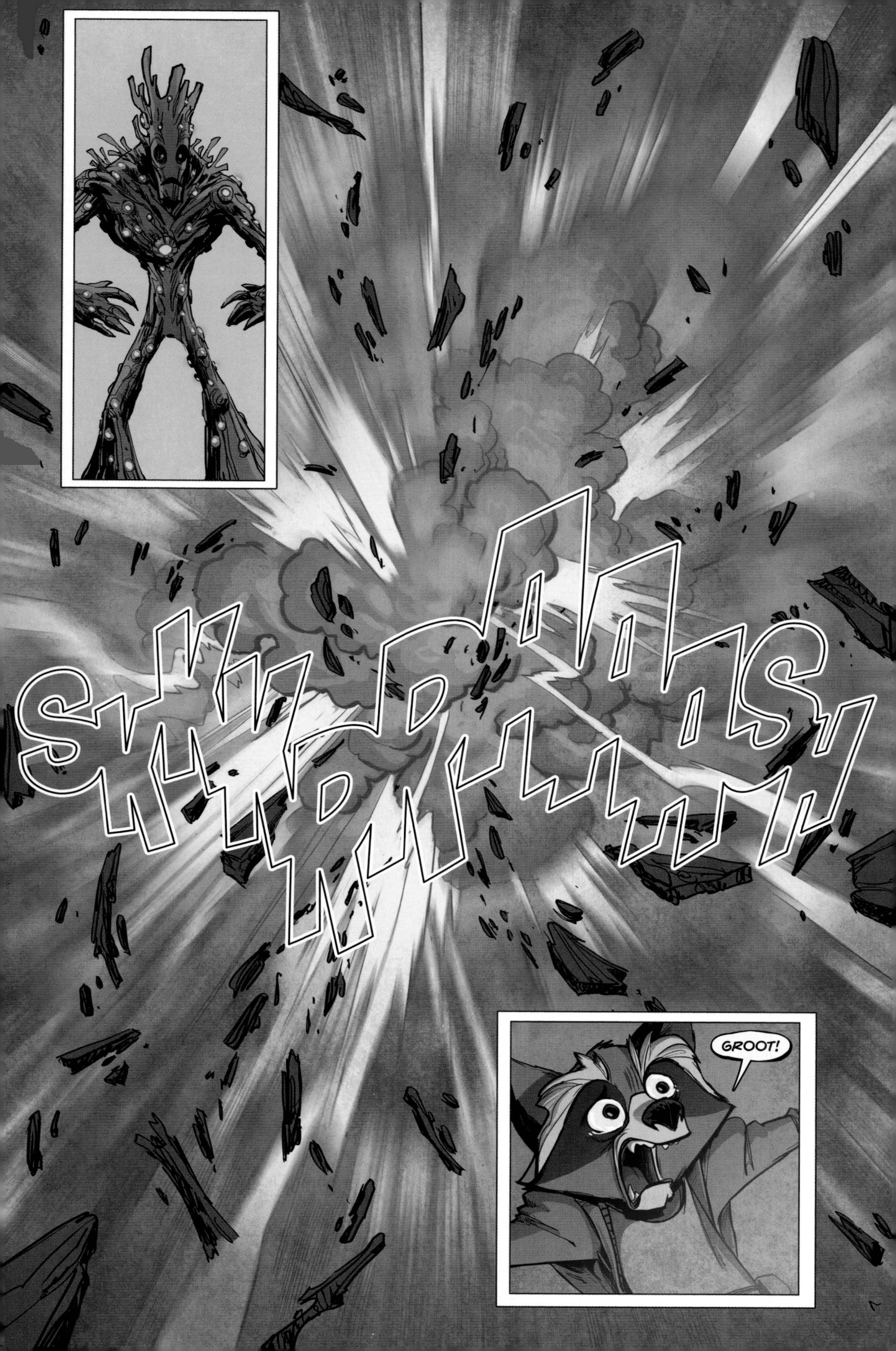
GROOT!

FWOOOOOSH

TORCH EVERY-THING.

HE GROWS BACK FAST. I DON'T WANT A SPLINTER LEFT!

AND SHOW HIS FRIENDS THE AIRLOCK. THEY'RE NOT WORTH ANYTHING.

WHAT ARE YOU DOING?

THE ONLY THING I CAN DO...

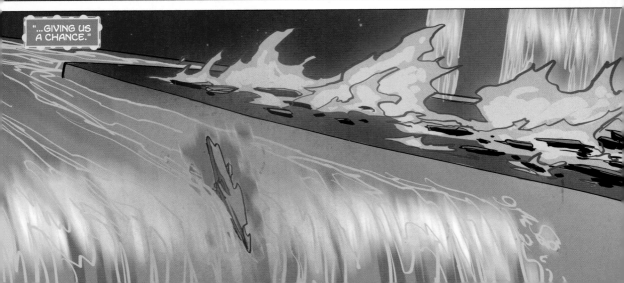

"...GIVING US A CHANCE."

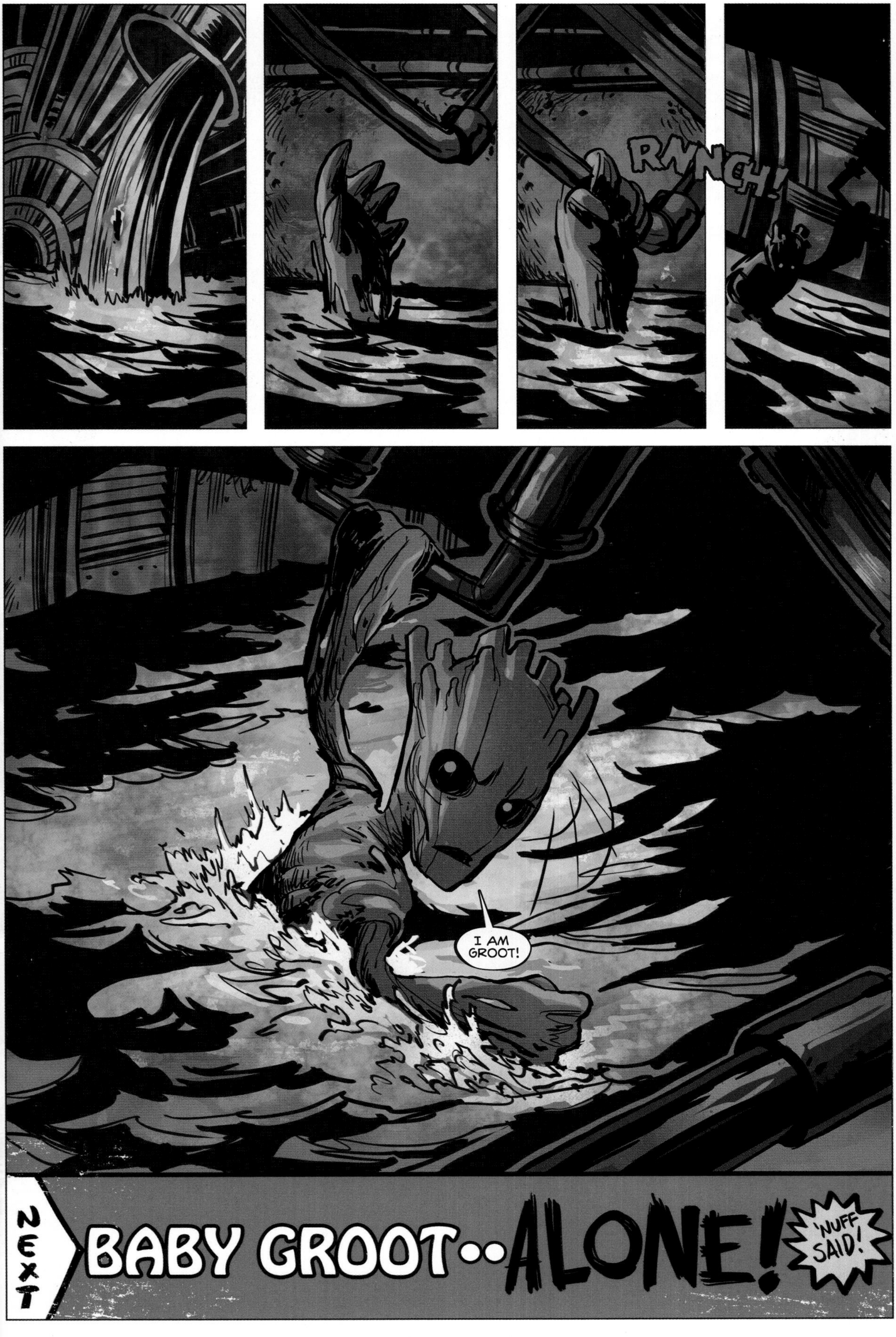
RANNCH!
I AM GROOT!
NEXT
BABY GROOT··ALONE!
'NUFF SAID!

GUARDIANS OF THE GALAXY

GROOT

COLLECT THEM ALL!

Set of 6 Hardcover Books ISBN:
978-1-5321-4076-1

Hardcover Book ISBN
978-1-5321-4077-8

Hardcover Book ISBN
978-1-5321-4078-5

Hardcover Book ISBN
978-1-5321-4079-2

Hardcover Book ISBN
978-1-5321-4080-8

Hardcover Book ISBN
978-1-5321-4081-5

Hardcover Book ISBN
978-1-5321-4082-2